The Rubbish Dump Whale

ISBN
978-0-9931527-4-0

Published by Generation 2050
www.generation2050project.org

As you may have guessed,
the Rubbish Dump Whale lived
in a rubbish dump.

How could a whale live in
a rubbish dump? You ask.

Well, because it wasn't always a rubbish
dump,

it used to be the sea,
but people made too much rubbish and that was
the only place left to put it.

The oceans were so full of rubbish

that there, wasn't
any room left
for the animals.

Jellyfish shaped bags and tin cans that looked like crabs bobbed and floated down to the sand.

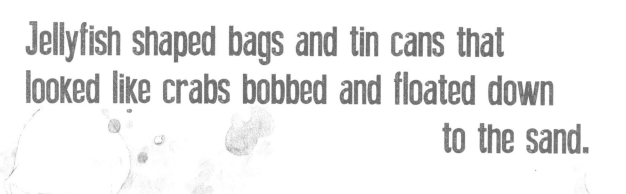

Old Chocolate bar wrappers collected and shoaled like fish would do before the sea became a rubbish dump for people's junk.

The Rubbish Dump Whale spent his days following the trails of rubbish and gobbling up everything from plastic cups to rubber ducks.

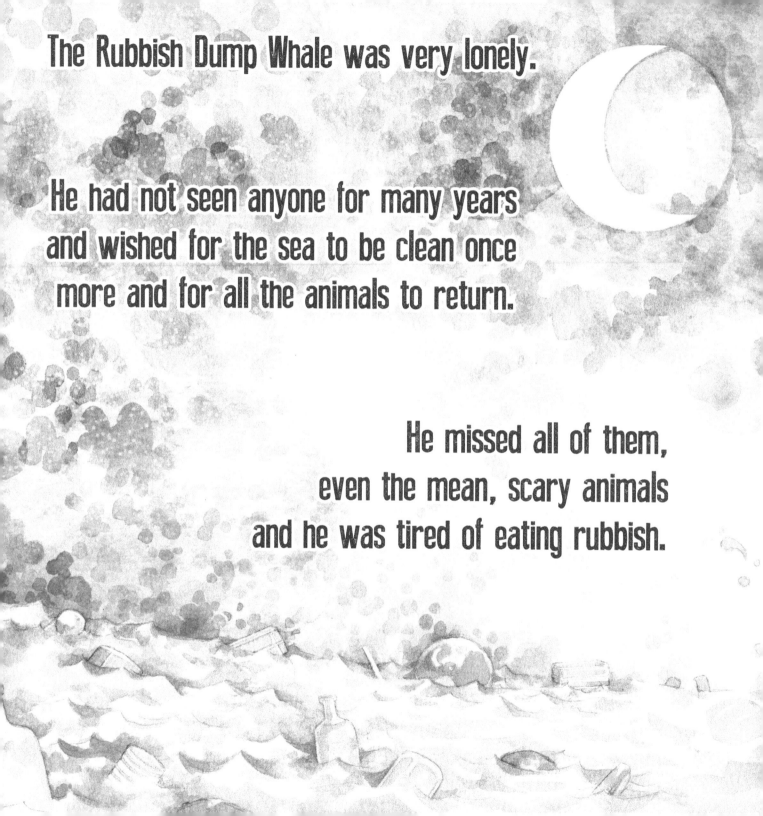

The Rubbish Dump Whale was very lonely.

He had not seen anyone for many years
and wished for the sea to be clean once
more and for all the animals to return.

He missed all of them,
even the mean, scary animals
and he was tired of eating rubbish.

As day turned to night and the stars twinkled in the sky, the Rubbish Dump Whale jumped as high as he could to reach them.

He thought that if he could live among the stars he would be free of the rubbish.

So he jumped and he jumped all night long until a voice boomed across the dump.

'Hey! Would you keep it down? Some of us are trying to get some sleep!'

The Rubbish Dump Whale was very confused.
'Did I say that?' he wondered to himself.
'No! I did,' the voice boomed again.
'I'm not rubbish! I'm an octopus! Ollie's the name,'
he said and slowly
slid out from the bottle to reveal his tentacles.

'An octopus! That is amazing!
I thought all the other animals were gone,'
the Rubbish Dump Whale
shrieked with excitement.

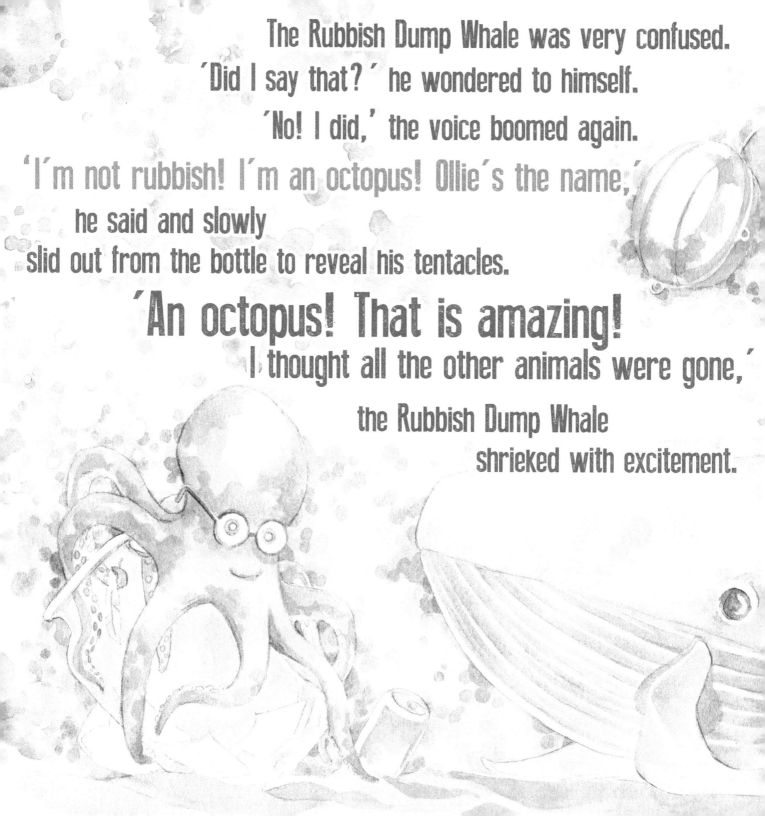

'They will be soon if we don't do something,'
said Ollie the Octopus.

'What can we do? We can't stop the rubbish,'
said the whale sadly.

'We can try! I've been writing messages for the people and putting them in bottles! Maybe if they understand they won't put their rubbish in the sea.'

'What a fantastic idea!'

'The only problem is that I live so far away from the land and I can only carry one bottle at a time.'

'I can help you Ollie. I can't write but I can swim very fast. I can deliver your messages.'

'Excellent! Let's get cracking!'
Ollie beamed enthusiastically.
They worked together through the night.
The Rubbish Dump Whale collected bottles
and Ollie wrote the letters.

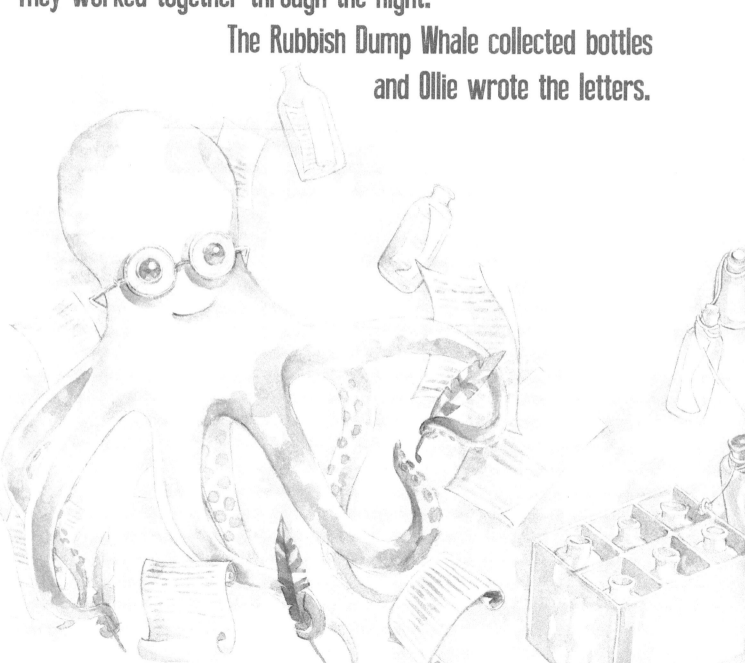

When the sun started to rise above the horizon, they set off for land.

They were making great progress as the Rubbish Dump Whale
crashed through the trash with Ollie on his back, when suddenly
they heard a bird crying for help.

she squawked.

She was tangled up in an old fishing net
and trying desperately to keep her beak above the waves.

Without giving it a second thought,
the Rubbish Dump Whale rushed to her rescue.

He dived under the waves
and surfaced with the bird and net on his back.

Ollie put his 8 arms to good use
and helped untangle the bird
from the fishing net.

The tired bird caught her breath, then said,

'Thank you so much for helping me.'

'People dump old fishing nets all over the sea
and birds get caught whilst they are searching for fish,'

sighed Ollie.

´Someone should really do something about that,´ said the bird.

´We are on our way to tell the people to stop right
now,´ said the Rubbish Dump Whale.

´Can I help you?
I know the way to land!´
she chirped.

'Lead the way,' Ollie gestured.

And with that
they all set off for land.

Once they reached the shore,
the bird flew inland
to drop the bottles over gardens.

Meanwhile, neither the Rubbish Dump Whale
nor Ollie the Octopus
could go on land like the bird,
so they worked together
to deliver their share of bottles.

Ollie placed the bottles on the
Rubbish Dump Whales' blow-hole,
which he catapulted on to the beach
using jets of water.

As the day drew to a close,
the unlikely trio gathered to watch the sunset
and reflect on all their hard work.

'It's not over yet,
we need to tell all the people
in all the countries of the world,'
said Ollie.

'We better get started then,'
said the bird.

'Where next?'
'America!'

And off they went,
a bird, a whale and an octopus,
to save the world!

Will you help them?

Dear ground animals
that look like this.

Please stop putting
all your stuff
that looks like this
in our home.

Love, Me

Have you ever
wondered where
the plastic stickers
on apples end up?

Hello Humans
Please stop making so
much plastic stuff
because it takes
hundreds of years
to break down
and it tastes rubbish1
From The Animals

SAVE THE PLANET.
RE-USE YOUR PLASTIC
BAGS AND BOTTLES.

Please tell your Mummy or
Daddy that recycling your
rubbish is very important
because if you keep making
more and more rubbish there
will not be any room left.
Recycling means that old stuff
is made in to new stuff instead
of being thrown away in a
rubbish dump.
Look for this picture
which means you
can recycle your stuff.

Dear 1 person,

If the one person reading this letter
stops using plastic shopping bags
and uses a reusable shopping bag
instead, you will save our home (the
ocean) from 22,000 plastic bags
over your life-time!
We would really appreciate
your help,
Love, 1 Rubbish Dump Whale

DEAR PEOPLE,

PLEASE DON'T BUY
THiNGS WiTH LOTS
OF PLASTIC PACK-
AGING.

LOVE THE SEA ANi-
MALS XX

Did you know...

It takes one thousand years
for a plastic bag to decompose
(break down).

There is a garbage patch in the
Pacific Ocean twice the size of the
United Kingdom!

Humans use 10 billion plastic bags
every week worldwide.

100 00

sea animals are killed every year because
of plastic pollution.

1 million sea birds die every
year from plastic pollution.

2 million plastic bottles
are used every day
in the United Kingdom.

Plastic is not a natural material so it can't break down and return to the Earth to make new
things like natural materials do. Plastic is made by people and actually becomes more dangerous as it breaks down because it binds to dangerous chemicals in the water and small animals
can eat it, which can kill them or animals that eat them.

PLANET   PEOPLE   ANIMALS

Generation 2050 is a social enterprise which publishes ethical childrens stories and educational materials to encourage and inspire a generation of socially and environmentally conscious citizens.

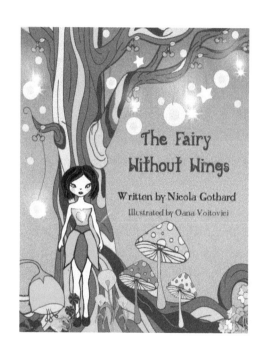

The Fairy
Without Wings

Written by Nicola Gothard
Illustrated by Oana Voitovici

Max & Bertie

BRING BACK BEES

Written by Nicola Gothard
Illustrated by Oana Voitovici

If you enjoyed this story please pass it on and check out our other titles available in both ebook and print formats from most major online book retailers.

@GEN2050

Lightning Source UK Ltd.
Milton Keynes UK
UKHW02f1240140118
316117UK00003B/8/P